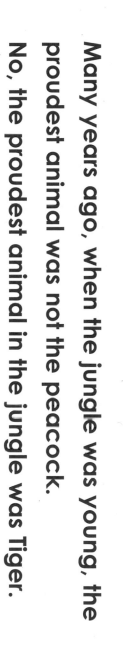

Many years ago, when the jungle was young, the proudest animal was not the peacock.

No, the proudest animal in the jungle was Tiger.

Tiger was proud of his long fangs.

Tiger was proud of his sharp claws and big paws.

Tiger was most proud of his beautiful golden coat.

Tiger was not afraid of any animal in the jungle, except Water Buffalo. Water Buffalo was big and strong. He had powerful horns on his head. One morning Tiger saw Water Buffalo hooked to a plow and made to work in the fields. Tiger was confused.

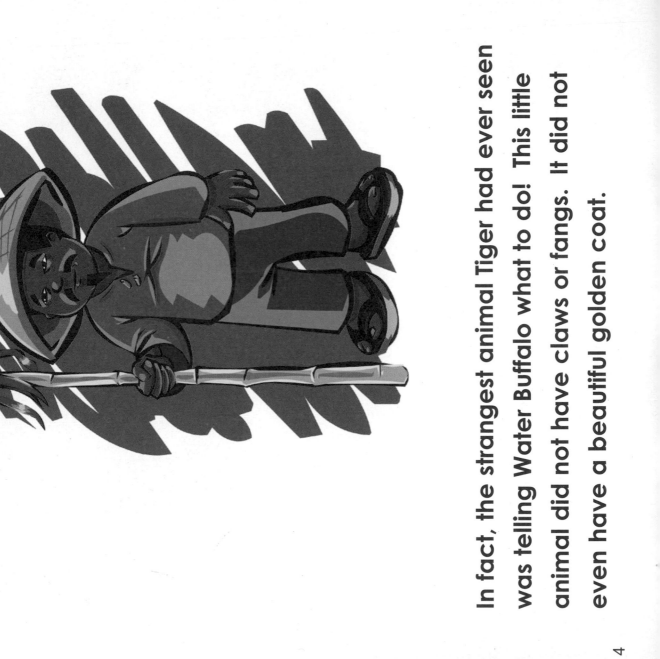

In fact, the strangest animal Tiger had ever seen was telling Water Buffalo what to do! This little animal did not have claws or fangs. It did not even have a beautiful golden coat.

Later, Tiger asked, "Water Buffalo, why do you work for that strange little animal? It does not have any claws or fangs, and it does not have a beautiful golden coat."

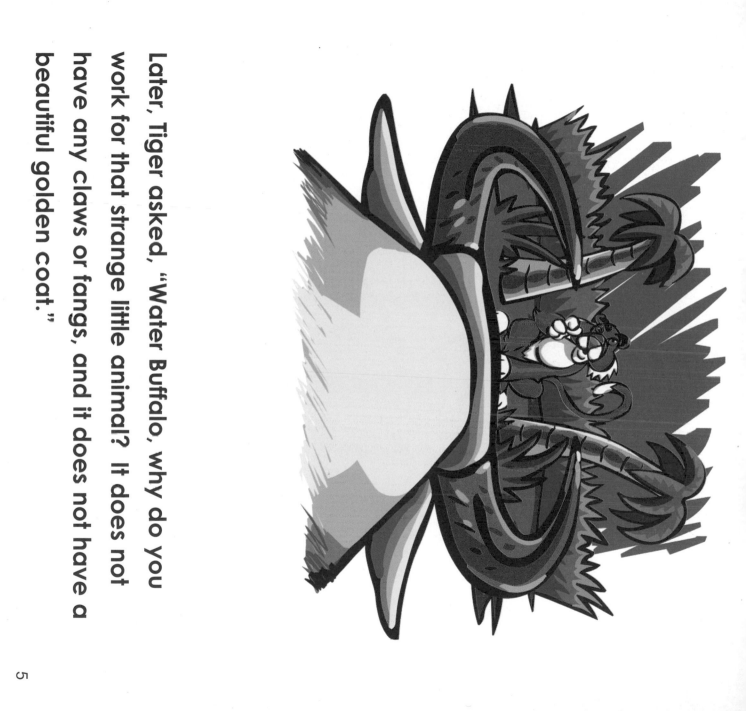

Water Buffalo shook his head and said to Tiger, "You do not understand, Tiger. That animal is Man, and he does not need claws or fangs, or even a golden coat. Man has wisdom."

Tiger said, "Well then, I must get some wisdom."
Water Buffalo just shook his head and walked away.

The next morning when Man was on his way to work, Tiger jumped out and said, "Stop, Man!"

Man looked at Tiger and said, "What do you want, Tiger?"

"I know you have wisdom and with your wisdom you make Water Buffalo work for you. I want your wisdom. Give me your wisdom," said Tiger.

Man looked at Tiger and said, "Tiger, wisdom is not something I can give you."

Tiger just shook his head and said, "Yes, you can. Give me your wisdom or I will eat you."

Man thought and said, "Okay, no problem, Tiger. I will give you my wisdom, but I left it back at my house. I will go and get it."

Man started to walk off but changed his mind. He said to Tiger, "Oh Tiger, mighty Tiger, I am afraid to go get you the wisdom. By the time I get back, you will have eaten all my goats. Would you mind if I tied you to this big tree? Just by the tip of your tail? Then you cannot get to my goats."

Tiger thought for a minute and said, "Okay, Man. Just tie the tip of my tail to the tree. Then go get the wisdom."

Man took a few steps and then turned around. He said, "Oh mighty Tiger, I am still afraid you may get hungry. Your powerful claws will cut the rope and you will eat all my goats."

"Look, Man, if it will make you feel better, tie my paws to the tree," spoke Tiger. So Man took the rope and tied Tiger tightly to the tree.

"Now go get my wisdom," said Tiger.
Man left again but turned back one more time.

Man said, "Tiger, mighty Tiger, your mighty fangs will rip these ropes and you will eat all my goats."

"All right already, just tie my head to the tree," said Tiger.

Behind Tiger's back, Man quietly led his goats away.

Tiger waited all day. Many animals walked by and saw Tiger tied to the tree. Tiger told them to go away and proudly said, "Man is bringing wisdom to me."

At last, Water Buffalo walked by and said, "Tiger, what have you gotten yourself into?" Water Buffalo just shook his head and walked away.

Tiger waited and waited and waited. Then Tiger said to himself, "I am getting a little hungry. Hmmm. Maybe I will eat just one of those goats."

Tiger was tied very tightly to the tree. Tiger yelled, "Come back, Man! I am getting very hungry."

Tiger pulled, and he pulled, and he pulled, and he pulled.
Finally, Tiger broke free.

The ropes had burned stripes into his coat. Tiger said, "Where are all the goats? Where is Man? Where is my wisdom?"

"I do not have wisdom," said Tiger, "but I still have my claws, my fangs, and my beautiful golden coat."

Tiger was thirsty, so he went to the lake for a drink. When he saw himself in the water, Tiger screamed, "Oh, my beautiful golden coat! It is covered with stripes."

All of the animals saw the stripes, but only Water Buffalo spoke.

He said, "Hey, Tiger, nice stripes. Heh, heh, heh, heh, heh."

Tiger, embarrassed by his stripes, slinks around and
hides in the shadows.

He is still searching for wisdom.